**For Neil with love and affection
and for Wendy
M.B.**

First published in Great Britain in 1991 by
Simon & Schuster Young Books
Campus 400
Maylands Avenue
Hemel Hempstead
Herts. HP2 7EZ

Reprinted in 1992 and 1994

Set in Melior Roman by Goodfellow & Egan Ltd., Cambridge
Printed and bound in Belgium by Proost International Book Production

British Library Cataloguing in Publication Data
Blackman, Malorie
  That New Dress
  I. Title II. Nest James, Rhian
  823.914 [f]

ISBN 0 7500 0442 8
ISBN 0 7500 0443 6 Pbk

That New Dress

Written by
Malorie Blackman

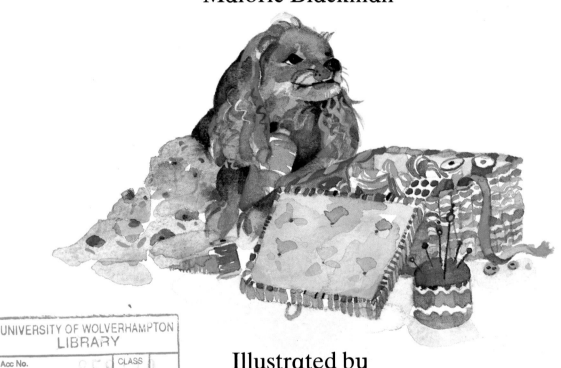

Illustrated by
Rhian Nest James

SIMON & SCHUSTER
YOUNG BOOKS

Wendy was sad.
Wendy was mad.
"Grandma, I haven't got a dress to wear to
Jennifer's party tomorrow," Wendy said.
Grandma rocked slowly; backwards, forwards,
backwards, forwards.
"Your mum's making you a dress," Grandma replied.

"I want that dress in Mr. MacKenzie's shop window,"
Wendy stamped her foot.
"But the dress your mum's making will be the
prettiest dress at the party," Grandma said.
And Grandma rocked; backwards, forwards,
backwards, forwards – and smiled.

Wendy pouted.
Wendy shouted.
"Dad, can I have the dress in Mr. MacKenzie's shop?"
Wendy asked. "I'd look really good in that dress."
Dad dug his spade into his vegetable garden;
in, out, in, out.

"But you'll look great in the dress your mum
is making you," Dad said.
"But I want the one in Mr. MacKenzie's shop,"
Wendy said.
But Dad didn't seem to hear her.
He dug his spade into the soil;
in, out, in, out – and he smiled.

Wendy sighed.
Wendy cried.
"Ben," Wendy said to her brother, "all my friends
are going to be at the party tomorrow and
I haven't got a dress to wear."
Ben threw his ball against the wall and caught it
as it fell; up, down, up, down.
"Who cares about a silly dress," Ben said.

"I'd be the happiest girl there if I had
the dress in Mr. MacKenzie's shop," Wendy said.
"Who cares about that?" Ben shrugged.
And he threw his ball against the wall again;
up, down, up, down — and Ben smiled.

Wendy breathed deep.
And had a good weep.
Doodle the dog was chasing her tail;
round and round.

"Oh, Doodle," Wendy said. "I want that dress
in Mr. MacKenzie's shop so much."
"Woof!" Doodle barked.
And she chased her tail again;
round and round.

Wendy went for a walk.
Past the neighbours' houses and down the street.
She walked to Mr. MacKenzie's shop and
stopped outside the window.

There was her dress.
The dress she wanted so badly.
She wanted it more than strawberry sweets and
liquorice treats.
She wanted it more than sherbet drops and icicle pops.
She wanted it more than anything.

"Hello Wendy," said Mr. MacKenzie.
"Have you come to buy a dress?"
Wendy shook her head.
"These are very popular," Mr. MacKenzie said.
"Shall I save you one?"
Wendy shrugged.
She was too sad to speak.

That night Wendy stared out at the moon.
"Please, please let Mum and Dad buy me the dress
in Mr. MacKenzie's window," Wendy said.
And the moon seemed to wink back.

The next day, when it was time to go
to Jennifer's party, Mum smiled.
"Here's your new dress, Wendy."

Wendy was sad and mad and
pouted and shouted and sighed and cried
all at once.
"I don't want that stupid dress!"

"You can wear this dress or not go to Jennifer's
party at all," Mum said.
"Make up your mind."

So Wendy wore the dress.
And she HATED it.

Mum walked Wendy along the road
to Jennifer's house.
Wendy looked down at the ground,
and frowned and frowned.

She didn't even look up when they passed
Mr. MacKenzie's shop.

"Here we are at last," Mum said.
"Hi! Wendy, you're just in time," said Jennifer's dad.
"We're playing hide-and-seek in the garden.
Come on! You can search for everyone!"

First Wendy found Jenny,

then Peter,

then Fay,

then Vijay and Simon,

and Susan and May.

Then Roma and Eddie and Heather together.

Hey! that was funny. Wow! that was odd.
All the girls at the party were like peas in a pod.
They each wore the dress that she'd wanted to wear.
So hers was the only *different* dress there.

Wendy laughed as they played inside
the house and smiled as each said,
"Your dress is pretty . . ."
"Your dress is best . . ."
"It looks really good . . ."
"I like your new dress!"
"Thank you," said Wendy.
"My mum made it for me."

Soon Jennifer's dad called out, "Tea time!".
Jennifer blew out the candles on her birthday cake
and her dad took a photograph.
"Say cheese! Smile please!"

Wendy was glad,
And no longer sad.
As they walked home, Wendy skipped
beside her mum.
"Thanks for the dress," Wendy grinned.
"You're welcome," Mum replied.
And Mum smiled.

Here are some more picture books published by Simon & Schuster Young Books for you to enjoy:

Six Dinner Sid
Written and illustrated by Inga Moore

Sid the cat has six owners, who all believe he is theirs, and theirs alone. As long as he has six dinners a day, Sid is happy. But when Sid's owners find out, they are furious!

Fish Fish Fish
Written by Georgie Adams - Illustrated by Brigitte Willgoss

Stripy fish and spotty fish, shy fish and bold fish, round fish and square fish - you'll find them all in this colourful introduction to the world of fish.

A Mother for Choco
Written and illustrated by Keiko Kasza

Choco desperately wants a mother, but he can't find anyone who looks at all like him. Then Mrs Bear asks him what a mother would do - and little Choco finds the answer is staring him in the face!

Bear's Christmas Surprise
Written by Elizabeth Winthrop - Illustrated by Patience Brewster

While playing hide-and-seek with Mrs Duck, Bear finds a pile of boxes all wrapped up in Christmas paper. Bear can't help taking a little peek...

Grandpa's Handkerchief
Written by Dorothy Clark - Illustrated by Siobhan Dodds

Grandpa uses a different handkerchief for every task, from bandaging a knee to reminding himself of a birthday and, of course, for AH-AH-CHOO!

The Jolly Witch
Written by Dick King-Smith - Illustrated by Frank Rodgers

Cuddly Mrs Jolly is a school caretaker by day and a witch by night. This Halloween, Mrs Jolly is determined to win in the grand broomstick race...

Available from all good bookshops

For more information please contact The Sales Department, Simon & Schuster Young Books, Campus 400, Maylands Avenue, Hemel Hempstead HP2 7EZ. Telephone (0442) 881900 - Fax (0442) 214467

PRINTED IN BELGIUM BY
proost
INTERNATIONAL BOOK PRODUCTION